Ladybird  Readers

The Enormous
Crocodile

Series Editor: Sorrel Pitts
Text adapted by R.J. Corrall
Activities written by Catrin Morris
With thanks to Michelle Porte-Davies

LADYBIRD BOOKS

UK | USA | Canada | Ireland | Australia
India | New Zealand | South Africa

Ladybird Books is part of the Penguin Random House group of companies
whose addresses can be found at global.penguinrandomhouse.com.
www.penguin.co.uk www.puffin.co.uk www.ladybird.co.uk

Penguin
Random House
UK

Text adapted from *The Enormous Crocodile*,
first published by Puffin Books, 1978
This version published by Ladybird Books Ltd, 2020

ROALD
DAHL

Printed in China

A CIP catalogue record for this book is available from the British Library

ISBN: 978-0-241-36816-9

All correspondence to:
Ladybird Books
Penguin Random House Children's
80 Strand, London WC2R 0RL

MIX
Paper from
responsible sources
FSC
www.fsc.org
FSC® C018179

Ladybird 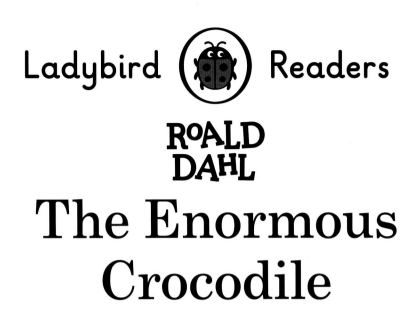 Readers

ROALD DAHL

The Enormous Crocodile

Based on the original title
by Roald Dahl
Illustrated by Quentin Blake

The Enormous Crocodile

Trunky, the elephant

Muggle-Wump, the monkey

The Roly-Poly Bird

bang

bench

bite

fair

jungle

roundabout

see-saw

tail

wood/wooden

In the biggest, brownest river in the jungle, there were two crocodiles. One was an Enormous Crocodile.

"For my lunch today," the
Enormous Crocodile said,
"I want to catch a nice little child!"

"You can't do that!" said the other crocodile.

"Yes, I can," said the Enormous Crocodile. "I have clever ideas."

Then, he swam across the river.

In the jungle, he met Trunky, the elephant, and bit him on the leg.

"Ow!" said Trunky. "What are you doing here?"

"I have clever ideas," said the Enormous Crocodile.

"I want to find a child to eat,
With nice arms and legs
and feet!"

"You horrible crocodile!"
said Trunky.

The Enormous Crocodile laughed.
"Goodbye!" he said.

Soon, he met Muggle-Wump, the monkey.

"Hello," said Muggle-Wump. "Where are you going?"

"I have clever ideas," said the Enormous Crocodile.

*"I very much enjoy
A lunch of little girl or boy!"*

"You can't eat a child!"
said Muggle-Wump.

"Yes, I can," said the crocodile.

"You horrible crocodile!"
said Muggle-Wump.

"I eat monkeys, too!" the crocodile
said, and he bit Muggle-Wump's tree.

Soon, the Enormous Crocodile met the Roly-Poly Bird.

"Hello there!" said the Roly-Poly Bird. "We don't often see you here in the jungle."

"Ah," said the crocodile. "I have clever ideas."

"I hope they are nice ideas," said the Roly-Poly Bird.

"Oh, yes!" said the crocodile.

*"They're very small and very sweet.
They are the greatest things to eat!"*

"I know! Fruit!" said the
Roly-Poly Bird.

The Enormous Crocodile laughed.
"Crocodiles don't eat fruit!" he said.
"We eat boys and girls!
And Roly-Poly Birds, too!"

He bit the bird's tail, but the bird
flew out of the tree.

21

The Enormous Crocodile came out of
the jungle and went into a playground.

"Now for Clever Idea Number One!"
he said.

He found some wood, and he put it on the grass. Then, he got on it and stayed very straight.

When the children came out of school, they were excited.

"Look! A new see-saw!" they said.

"When a child sits on my head," the Enormous Crocodile thought, "I can eat their feet!"

25

Then, Muggle-Wump ran out of the trees.

"That's not a see-saw!" he said. "It's the Enormous Crocodile, and he wants to eat you!"

The children ran, and Muggle-Wump ran, too.

Now, the Enormous Crocodile was hungry. He came to a fair, and he saw a roundabout.

"Here's Clever Idea Number Two!" he said.

When no one could see him, he went and stood on the roundabout.

"I want to go on that horse!" said a girl

"I want to go on that old wooden crocodile," said a boy.

Then, the Roly-Poly Bird flew down. "It isn't a wooden crocodile," he said. "It's the Enormous Crocodile, and he wants to eat you!"

The children ran from the Enormous Crocodile.

Now, the Enormous Crocodile was
VERY hungry. He came to a
picnic place.

"Here's Clever Idea Number Three!" he said.

He put some flowers on a table and stood next to it like a bench.

Soon, four children came for
a picnic.

"Let's sit at the table with the
flowers!" they said.

Then, Trunky ran out of the jungle.
"That isn't a bench!" he said.
"It's the Enormous Crocodile, and
he wants to eat you!"

The children ran from the
Enormous Crocodile.

Trunky ran to the
Enormous Crocodile. He held
his tail and threw him around
and around.

He threw him faster . . .
and faster . . .

and FASTER.

Then, the Enormous Crocodile went up, up . . .
Above the clouds,
Past the moon,
Past the stars.

He went into the sun and went BANG, like a hot sausage!

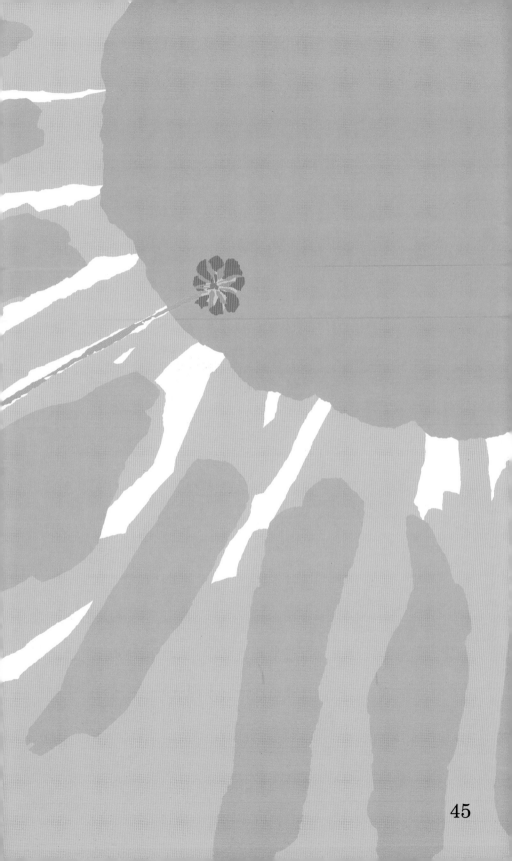

Activities

The key below describes the skills practiced in each activity.

✏️ Spelling and writing

📖 Reading

💬 Speaking

❓ Critical thinking

✴️ Preparation for the Cambridge Young Learners exams

1 Look, match, and write the words. 📖 ✏️

1 | The Enormous ———— Bird

| Trunky, ———— Crocodile

2

3 | Muggle-Wump, | the elephant

4 | The Roly-Poly | the monkey

1 The Enormous Crocodile

2

3

4

2 Find the words.

lirbenchhifairhrjungleosjtailgrowoodenwghrioroundaboutebiteh

bench
bite
fair
jungle
roundabout
tail
wooden

3 Look and read. Choose the correct words and write them on the lines. 📖 ✏️ ⭐

The Roly-Poly Bird | Muggle-Wump | Trunky | The Enormous Crocodile

1 He's blue and he can fly. → The Roly-Poly Bird

2 He's very big and green.

3 He's big and gray.

4 He's brown and lives in a tree.

4 Look at the pictures. Put a by the correct words.

1  **a** byt ☐
b bite ✓

2  **a** bench ☐
b bensh ☐

3  **a** aboutround ☐
b roundabout ☐

4  **a** saw-see ☐
b see-saw ☐

5  **a** tail ☐
b tale ☐

6  **a** fair ☐
b fare ☐

5 Ask and answer the questions with a friend.

In the biggest, brownest river in the jungle, there were two crocodiles. One was an Enormous Crocodile.

"For my lunch today," the Enormous Crocodile said, "I want to catch a nice little child!"

1

How many crocodiles are there in the picture?

There are two.

2 Where are they?

3 What time of day is it?

4 What does the Enormous Crocodile want to do?

6 Circle the correct sentences.

1

    a The crocodile swam across the river.

    b The crocodile swam under the river.

2

    a The crocodile bit Trunky on the leg.

    b Trunky bit the crocodile on the tail.

3

    a The crocodile met the Roly-Poly Bird.

    b The crocodile met Muggle-Wump.

4

    a "I have clever ideas," said the crocodile.

    b "I don't have clever ideas," said the crocodile.

7 Read the text. Choose the correct words and write them next to 1—4.

can't eat   eat   can   bit

"You ¹ .... can't eat .... a child!"

said Muggle-Wump.

"Yes, I ² ....," said the

Enormous Crocodile.

"You horrible crocodile!"

said Muggle-Wump.

"I ³ .... monkeys, too!"

the Enormous Crocodile said, and he

⁴ .... Muggle-Wump's tree.

8 Write the questions. Then, write the answers. 📖 ✏️

1 (Roly-Poly Bird) (crocodile) (does)

(meet) (the) (the) (Where) (?)

Question: Where does the crocodile meet the Roly-Poly Bird?

Answer: In the jungle.

2 (clever) (has) (ideas) (Who) (?)

Question: ....

Answer: ....

3 (want) (eat) (does) (crocodile)

(the) (What) (to) (?)

Question: ....

....

54   Answer: ....

9 Circle the correct words.

"Oh, yes!" said the crocodile.

*"They're very small and very sweet.
They are the greatest things to eat!"*

"I know! Fruit!" said the
Roly-Poly Bird.

The Enormous Crocodile laughed.
"Crocodiles don't eat fruit!" he said.
"We eat boys and girls!
And Roly-Poly Birds, too!"

He bit the bird's tail, but the bird
flew out of the tree.

20 21

1 "They're very **big /(small)**and
very sweet."

2 "They are the **greatest / worst**
things to eat!"

3 "I know! **Chocolate!" / Fruit!"**
said the Roly-Poly Bird.

4 The Enormous Crocodile laughed.
"Crocodiles **don't eat / eat** fruit!"
he said.

10 **Write the missing letters.**

coghiknndopr

1

cro C O dile

2

ele........ ....ant

3

mo........ ....ey

4

b........ ....d

5

ju........ ....le

6

wo........ ....en

11 Look and read. Write the correct words in the boxes.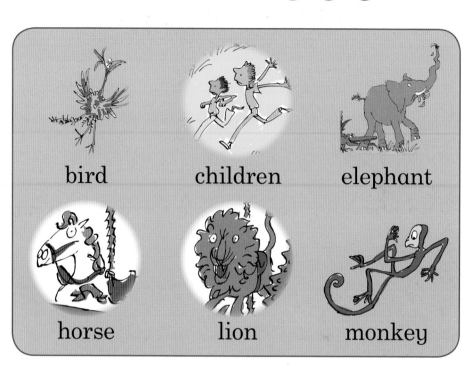

bird

children

elephant

horse

lion

monkey

At the fair	In the jungle
	bird

12 Work with a friend. Look at the pictures. One picture is different. How is it different? 🔘

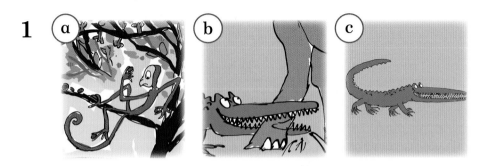

Picture a is different because the animal is a monkey and not a crocodile.

13 Write *from*, *into*, *next to*, or *out of*.

1  The bird flew
___out of___ the tree.

2  The children ran
_____ the
Enormous Crocodile.

3  He put some flowers
on a table and stood
_____ it.

4  Then, Trunky
ran _____
the jungle.

5  He went _____ the
sun and went BANG,
like a hot sausage!

14 Who said this?

the Enormous Crocodile   Trunky

Muggle-Wump   the Roly-Poly Bird

1 "I want to catch a nice little child!"

said <u>the Enormous Crocodile</u>.

2 "Ow! What are you doing here?"

said ....

3 "We don't often see you here in the

jungle," said ....

4 "Run! That's not a see-saw. It's the

Enormous Crocodile, and he wants

to eat you!" said ....

15 Write about your favorite place.
Why do you like it?

My favorite place is

16 **Circle the correct words.**

Trunky ran to the
Enormous Crocodile. He held
his tail and threw him around
and around.

36   37

1 Trunky ran to the

   a children.

   b Enormous Crocodile.

2 He held him by his

   a nose.

   b tail.

3 He threw him

   a around and around.

   b slower and slower.

Look and read. Write *true* or *false*.

Then, the Enormous Crocodile went
up, up . . .
Above the clouds,
Past the moon,
Past the stars.

42   43

1 The Enormous Crocodile
fell down.   *false*

2 He went above the clouds.   ....

3 He went past the sun.   ....

4 He went past the stars.   ....

5 He went BANG, like
a hot sausage!

Visit **www.ladybirdeducation.co.uk**
for more FREE Ladybird Readers resources

✓ Digital edition
  of every title*

✓ Audio tracks (US/UK)

✓ Answer keys

✓ Lesson plans

✓ Role-plays

✓ Classroom
  display material

✓ Flashcards

✓ User guides

Register and sign up to the newsletter to receive your
FREE classroom resource pack!